The FUNNY RIDE

A Follett JUST Beginning-To-Read Book

The FUNNY RIDE

Margaret Hillert

Illustrated by Jözef Sumichrast

FOLLETT PUBLISHING COMPANY
Chicago

Library of Congress Cataloging in Publication Data

Hillert, Margaret.
  The funny ride.

  (Follett just beginning-to-read books)
  SUMMARY: When his kite lifts him above the ground, a child takes a "funny ride" as he views what is on the ground and in the air.
  [1. Kites—Fiction. 2. Flight—Fiction]
I. Sumichrast, Jözef. II. Title.
PZ7.H558Fu [E] 80–20864
ISBN 0–695–41552–2 (lib. bdg.)
ISBN 0–695–31552–8 (pbk.)

First Printing

Oh, look.

Here is something big.

I can play with it.

I can make it go up.

See me run.
And see it go up.
Up, up, up.
Look at it go!

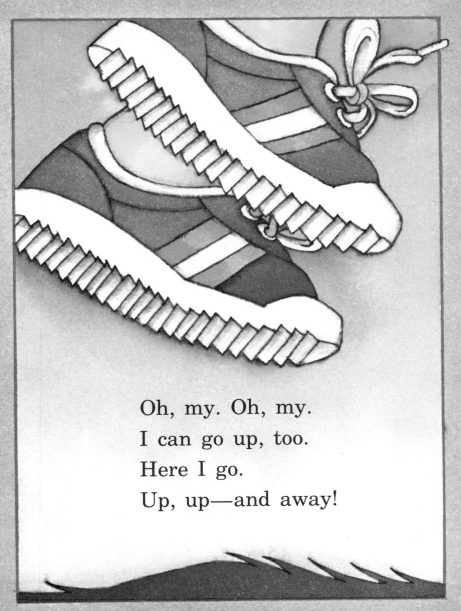

Oh, my. Oh, my.
I can go up, too.
Here I go.
Up, up—and away!

Look down. Look down.
I see cars.
I see my house.
I see my mother.

Mother, Mother.
Look up here.
Look at me go.
See what I can do.

No, no.
You can not do that.
Come down here to me.
I want you.

This is fun.

It is fun up here.

Look at me go.

Away, away, away.

Now I see my school.
It is a big one,
but it looks little.

And the boys and girls
look little, too.
That is funny.

14

Oh, oh.
Something is up here
with me now.
Something big, big, big.
Do you like it up here?

What will you do now?
Where will you go?
I want to go, too.

Oh, what is this?
I can not see in here.
I want to get out.

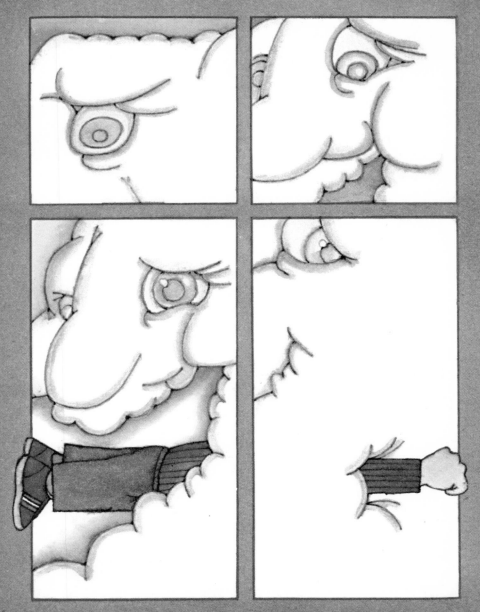

Now I am out.
But I am up, up, up.
Oh, my. Oh, my.

Look at that!
See it go down.
Down and down and down.

And now look.
I like to see this.
Red, yellow, blue.
How pretty it is!

Here is something pretty, too.
One, two, three pretty ones.
Oh, my. Oh, my.

And look at this.

See what this man can do.

He is good at it.

26

No, no.

Go away. Go away.

I do not want you to do this.

Look out. Look out.

This is not good for me.

Oh, oh.
Down I go.
What can I do?
Help! Help!

Mother, Mother.
Here I come.
Down,
    down,
        down.

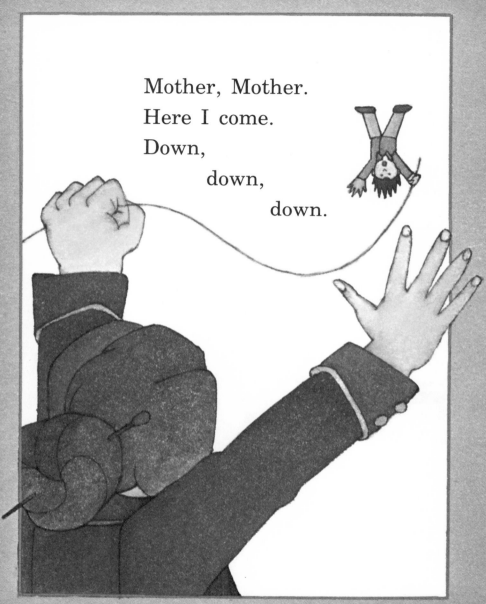

30

Oh, my.
What a ride!
What a funny, funny ride!

Margaret Hillert, author of many Follett JUST Beginning-To-Read Books, has been a first-grade teacher in Royal Oak, Michigan, since 1948.

The Funny Ride uses the 67 words listed below.

a	get	make	that
am	girls	man	the
and	go	me	this
at	good	mother	three
away		my	to
	he		too
big	help	no	two
blue	here	not	
boys	house	now	up
but	how		
		oh	want
can	I	one(s)	what
cars	in	out	where
come	is		will
	it	play	with
do		pretty	
down	like		yellow
	little	red	you
for	look(s)	ride	
fun		run	
funny			
		school	
		see	
		something	